PRESIDENT TAFT IS STUCK IN THE BATH

Mac Barnett   *illustrated by* **Chris Van Dusen**

CANDLEWICK PRESS

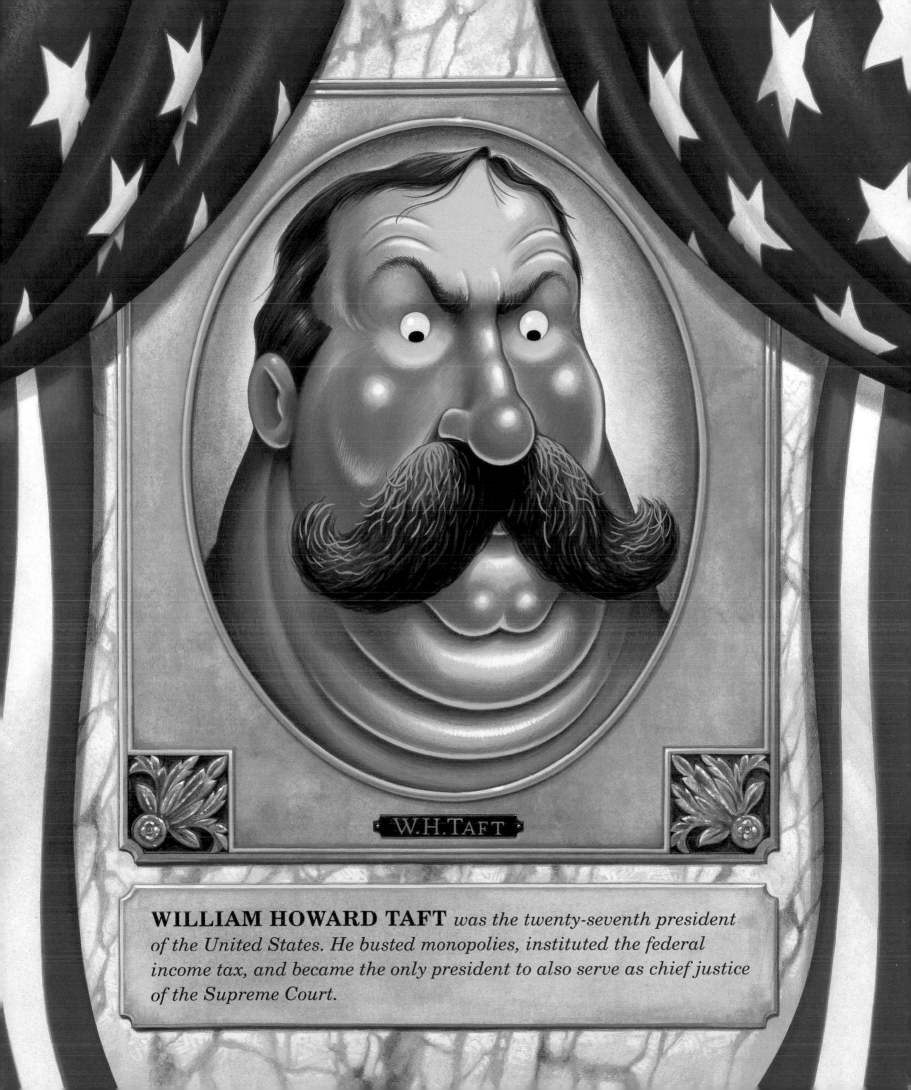

W.H. TAFT

WILLIAM HOWARD TAFT *was the twenty-seventh president of the United States. He busted monopolies, instituted the federal income tax, and became the only president to also serve as chief justice of the Supreme Court.*

But today President Taft is stuck in his bathtub.

"Blast!" said Taft. "This could be bad."

He squeezed and he shimmied.

He hefted and stretched.

He gripped the rim of the tub and attempted to lift himself. But it was no use: President Taft was stuck in the bath.

Taft took a deep breath and tugged his mustache.

"Think, Taft!" said Taft. "Use that big noggin and cook up a plan!"

Two hours passed.
The water got cold.
And President Taft was still stuck in the bath.

"I hope," said Taft, "that nobody notices I am missing."

Someone knocked at the door.

"Double blast!" said Taft. "Blast and drat!"

"Willy?"

Oh, dear. It was Taft's wife, the first lady of the United States of America.

"You've been in there a while. Is everything fine?"

Taft splashed in the bath.

"Yes, Nellie!" he said. "I'm just scrubbing my back!"

"I see," Nellie said. "Are you really quite sure?"

"Oh, blast!" shouted Taft. "Why can't a man have a nice quiet bath?"

Nellie said, "Sorry, Willy."

She sniffed. Taft felt bad.

"My love," said Taft, "I am stuck in the bath."

"So you are," said Nellie. She thought. "Well, perhaps—"

"It's a disaster!" said Taft.

"Yes, but perhaps—"

"Blast 'perhaps'!" shouted Taft. "We need action. A plan! Please be a sweetie and call the vice president."

The vice president came and stood by the tub.

"Well, Jim," said Taft, "I'm stuck in the bath."

"I see," said the V.P. "Well, you've called the right man. I'm ready to be sworn in as the president of the United States of America."

"Blast that!" bellowed Taft. "A preposterous plan."

"Perhaps—" said the first lady.

"Call the secretary of state!" shouted President Taft.

"Mr. Secretary," said Taft, "I'm stuck in the bath."

"Indeed," said the secretary of state. "Let me put this diplomatically. A man of great stature need not be of great girth, and so—"

"Blast, man!" shouted Taft. "Are you calling me fat?"

"No, sir!" The secretary of state was taken aback. "But certainly a diet, combined with calisthenics—"

"Blast diets!" said Taft. "I need something fast!"

"Should we swear me in as president now?" asked the vice president.

"Call the secretary of agriculture!" shouted President Taft.

"Mr. Secretary," said Taft, "I'm stuck in the bath."

"Hmm," said the secretary. "A huge vat of butter should do the trick. We'll have fifty farmers milk fifty cows. If Congress spends the night churning, we should have enough. We'll grease up your sides and the sides of the tub. Then it will be easy. You'll slide right out!"

"Blast butter!" said Taft. "As soon as I'm out, I'll just need a bath."

"Perhaps—" said the first lady.

"Call the secretary of war!" shouted President Taft.

"Mr. Secretary," said Taft, "I'm stuck in the bath."

"Yes," said the secretary. "We'll soon see to that."

"With what?" Taft asked.

"Dynamite!"

Taft was aghast.

"We just need a few sticks of TNT and a rather long fuse, and —*BOOM*— you'll be free! We'll blast this old tub into smithereens!"

"Blast blasting!" said Taft. "That's dangerous, man!"

"You'd be wearing a helmet," said the secretary of war.

"No!" shouted Taft.

"Don't you think *President James Schoolcraft Sherman* sounds catchy?" said the vice president.

"No!" shouted Taft.

"Perhaps—" said the first lady.

"Call the secretaries of the navy, treasury, and interior!" shouted President Taft.

"Send deep-sea divers into the tub!"
said the secretary of the navy.

"Throw money at the problem!"
said the secretary of the treasury.

"The answer is inside you,"
said the secretary of the interior.

"Blast that, that, and that!" shouted President Taft. "It is clear: I am unfit for office. A president cannot govern while stuck in a bath. Am I to be carried around this great nation in a tub, borne aloft on the backs of six young men like a princeling from antiquity?

"NO," bellowed Taft. "IT IS UN-AMERICAN."

Taft waved his right hand. "Fetch the chief justice. I will resign. Let's swear Sherman in."

"Wait!" said the first lady.

"Let's not be rash. There are eight of us here. Perhaps if we stopped using our brains and just used our arms, we could pull Willy out from the bath."

It was a pretty good plan. And so those eight great minds rolled up their sleeves, and they yanked and they tugged. At first Taft wouldn't budge. But then came a squeak, and a slap, and a snap, and just like that . . .

President Taft flew from the bath.

There were many glad cries. Taft kissed his wife. A celebration ensued,
and someone called in a band. There was dancing and snacks.
The secretary of state raised his glass.

"A toast," he said, "to President Taft. Worry not, great man:
One hundred years hence, no one will recall that you were stuck
in the bath. Our grandchildren's grandchildren will read of
your many great feats."

The crowd broke into applause.

"Speech! Speech!" they all said.

The band stopped. Taft cleared his throat.
Those gathered were rapt.

"Would somebody hand me a robe?" he asked.

And that's that.

Taft's White House tub, custom-built for the president by the J. L. Mott Iron Works of Trenton, New Jersey. Four men sit in the tub, and there looks to be room for at least two more.

Some people say President Taft got stuck in his bath on March 4, 1909, his inauguration day. Others say it happened later in his term. Depending on who's talking, it took two men to pry out the president, or four men, or four men plus a gallon of loblolly, which is butter mixed with lobster liver.

Of course, many say Taft never got stuck at all.

What follows is what we know for certain.